Arnie Lightning

CHRISTMAS ELF

Arnie Lightning Books

Copyright © 2015

Table of Contents

Tinsel the Christmas Elf

All of Santa's elves love Christmas, but there is no elf who loves Christmas quite as much as Tinsel does. Tinsel the elf has lived with Santa ever since Santa came to the North Pole, years and years ago. He is always filled to the brim with holiday cheer, no matter what time of the year it is.

Tinsel knows all the words to every Christmas carol ever written. He knows all the best ways to decorate a Christmas tree, bake the most delicious Christmas cookies, and bring Christmas cheer to the other elves and reindeer. Even when

Santa and Mrs. Claus are feeling sick or sad, Tinsel, with his joyful Christmas spirit, is sure to cheer them up every time.

Many years ago, Santa noticed Tinsel's remarkable Christmas spirit, and so he appointed him Chief Christmas Spirit Elf.

"What an honor!" gasped Tinsel. "Only...what does a Chief Christmas Spirit Elf do?"

Santa chuckled merrily. "Your job, Tinsel, will be to bring Christmas cheer to the children of the world. Each year, I will assign you to a different boy or girl who needs some holiday spirit, and it will be your job to cheer him or her up and to show them the true spirit of the season."

Tinsel was very excited to begin his job! His very first assignment involved a little boy named Timothy, who was too sad to enjoy Christmas because his father had died earlier that year.

Tinsel spent the whole Christmas season with Timothy. The two of them became great friends, and soon Timothy learned to laugh and have fun again. Because of this, he made even more new friends. Tinsel also helped Timothy learn to work in the woodcarver's shop that Timothy's father had owned and operated. Working in the shop made Timothy feel close to his father.

Just before Christmas, Tinsel found a carved wooden horse that Timothy's father had never had a chance to give Timothy. Late on Christmas Eve, Tinsel wrapped the horse in paper, tied it with a ribbon, and placed it beneath Timothy's Christmas tree. You can only imagine how touched and overjoyed Timothy was on Christmas morning when he discovered one last gift from his beloved father!

"Well done, Tinsel!" Santa exclaimed when Tinsel reported back to the North Pole that Christmas afternoon. "You brought Christmas cheer to Timothy when he needed it the most!"

Tinsel blushed and ducked his head, but Santa's praise made him feel wonderful.

As the years went by, Tinsel brought the Christmas Spirit to boys and girls in every country of the world. Because of his caring smile, warm heart, the spring in his step, and his incredible love for Christmas, the lives of children all around the globe were transformed. Tinsel couldn't think of any job he would like more than this one. For a Christmas-loving elf like him, what was better than spreading the true joy of Christmas all around the world?

Just for Fun Activity

Do you know of anyone who needs some extra-special cheering up this Christmas season? Follow Tinsel's good example and help spread some holiday spirit!

Christmas in Peru

"Tinsel!" bellowed Santa. "I have your special assignment for this year!"

Excitedly, Tinsel the Chief Christmas Spirit Elf danced toward Santa's office, humming a Christmas carol. Each year, Santa assigned Tinsel to a different boy or girl who was in need of some holiday cheer. It was Tinsel's job to cheer the child up and help him or her realize the true joy of the holidays.

"This year, I'm assigning you to a little girl named Maria Luisa," Santa told Tinsel. "She lives in Peru, and she's very unhappy because this year, her family in the United States won't be coming to visit like they usually do for the holidays."

"Poor Maria Luisa," said Tinsel.

Santa nodded. "She believes she won't be able to have a good Christmas without her relatives. It is your job to show her differently."

With a click of his magical elf heels, Tinsel transported himself to the city of Lima, Peru. Even though it was summer in Peru and the air was warm, the sights and sounds of Christmas were everywhere. Christmas decorations filled the city. Spanish Christmas carols blared from radios. Families decorated Christmas trees and enjoyed Christmas sweet bread and cups of spicy South-American hot chocolate.

It seemed to Tinsel that Maria Luisa must be the only child in the city who wasn't happy.

"Who are you?" she asked Tinsel in Spanish when he appeared in her bedroom. She had been crying, but now she dried her eyes.

"I'm Tinsel the Christmas Spirit Elf," Tinsel replied, also in Spanish. "I'm here to cheer you up, to get you back into the spirit of the holidays."

Maria Luisa sighed. "Don't bother," she said. "The holidays won't be any fun this year."

She told Tinsel all about how her family in the United States wouldn't be coming to visit. "Christmas won't be the same without them!" she complained.

"But what about the rest of your family, the ones who already live here in Peru?" Tinsel asked. "Aren't you grateful that they'll be here for Christmas? Don't you think it will make them feel bad to see you so unhappy?"

Maria Luisa looked as if she had never thought about that.

"I have an idea," Tinsel told her. "Why don't we work on making the Christmas season extra special this year, both for your family in Peru and for your family in the States?"

Maria Luisa wrinkled her nose in confusion. "How could we do that?"

"What if we made them all homemade gifts?" Tinsel suggested. "You can send a box full of special homemade gifts to your family in the United States, and you can put the rest under the tree for your family here!"

Immediately, Maria Luisa brightened. She loved crafts of every kind! With Tinsel's help, she went shopping for everything she would need. Then, she and Tinsel spent days making the perfect presents for all of Maria Luisa's relatives. They made scarves and bracelets and sock puppets and Christmas candy and homemade books and so much more. Tinsel helped Maria Luisa ship some of her presents out of the country. He helped her arrange the rest under her tree.

At midnight on Christmas Eve, they stood together, along with Maria Luisa's Peruvian family, and watched Christmas fireworks light up the night sky.

"Muchas gracias Tinsel!" Maria Luisa told him. "You brought me back my Christmas cheer!"

Tinsel the elf smiled very happily.

The Gift of Christmas

Each year, Santa gave Tinsel the elf the very important task of cheering up one little boy or girl who was especially in need of the Christmas spirit. Years ago, Santa had named Tinsel his Chief Christmas Spirit Elf, and Tinsel took his job very seriously. He loved Christmas more than anyone else, and nothing brought him greater joy than helping the children of the world learn to love Christmas just as much!

This year, Tinsel's assignment was to go to Chicago and help a little boy named Eddie. Eddie was a sad, lonely little kid who had been brought up in a family that treated Christmas just like any other day of the year. Because he didn't know any differently, Eddie pretended not to care about this. But deep down inside, he was envious of his friends and classmates, who talked nonstop about Christmas trees and Christmas presents and Santa and his reindeer.

You can imagine Eddie's surprise when Tinsel suddenly appeared in front of him one cold afternoon in early December. Eddie had been swinging on the swing set at a park near his house, but he almost fell off his swing when he saw Tinsel!

"Merry Christmas, Eddie!" Tinsel cried joyfully. He danced a happy jig, and the bells on the toes of his shoes jingled.

"I don't celebrate Christmas," Eddie said stubbornly.

"Why not?" Tinsel cried.

"Christmas is just another day of the year," Eddie mumbled.

"What if I told you I was a genuine Christmas Spirit elf, sent to you by none other than Santa himself?" Tinsel asked.

That got Eddie's attention. "Santa?" he couldn't help but gasp. "Why does Santa care about me?"

"Why shouldn't he?" Tinsel said. "You're one of the children of the world, and Santa loves you. He wants you to be happy, and so do I!" Tinsel jumped up, gabbing Eddie's hand. "Come on, Eddie! Let's go!"

Eddie's brown eyes brightened behind his glasses. "Go where?"

Tinsel didn't answer. He took Eddie straight to the nearest shopping mall, which was brimming with Christmas decorations, holiday music, and holiday sales. The candy store offered seasonal treats, and Eddie couldn't believe his eyes. Everything was so pretty and Christmassy!

Tinsel bought Eddie a peppermint hot chocolate and stood in line with him to sit on the mall Santa's lap. Eddie even had his picture taken with the mall Santa, something he had never done before!

The next afternoon, Tinsel met up with Eddie after he was done with school, and the two of them brought home a pretty Christmas wreath to hang on Eddie's front door. Tinsel could tell Eddie was really getting into the holiday spirit, and that made him very happy!

At first, Eddie's parents weren't sure how they felt about the wreath, but after a while, they decided it was pretty. Then, Eddie's mom even went so far as to suggest getting a Christmas tree! Tinsel went with her and Eddie and helped them pick the perfect one.

By the time Christmas came around, little Eddie and his whole family were finally enjoying the true happiness that Christmastime can bring. Eddie gave Tinsel a big hug and thanked him for helping them all learn to love the holidays at last!

Meghan's New Christmas Traditions

Tinsel the Chief Christmas Spirit Elf had been given the very important job of bringing Christmas cheer to boys and girls who especially needed some holiday spirit. This year, Santa assigned Tinsel to a little girl named Meghan, who was feeling particularly low during this happy season.

Over the past summer, Meghan's parents had a gotten a divorce. Now, even though Meghan would be spending Christmas Eve with her mom and Christmas Day with her dad, things weren't going to be the same. This would be the first Christmas she'd spend without both of her parents together.

When Tinsel arrived at Meghan's house, he found her sitting gloomily on the floor in her bedroom, trying to play with her stuffed animals. But she wasn't in the mood, and she kept staring sadly through the frosted windows.

Tinsel's arrival was the only thing that made her blink. Meghan was surprised to see a genuine Christmas elf standing right there in front of her! "Who are you?" she cried, jumping to her feet.

Tinsel said, "My name is Tinsel, and I'm here to help you have a happy holiday season."

"Not possible!" moaned Meghan, flopping onto her bed. "I'll never be happy ever again! Now that my parents are divorced, what's the point of even having Christmas in the first place?"

Tinsel patted her on the arm. "I know it's hard, Meghan," he said. "It will take a while for you to get used to things having changed, but you can do it. I believe in you, and Santa does, too."

Meghan sniffled. "Really?"

Tinsel smiled. "Yes, really."

Just knowing that seemed to help Meghan feel better. Tinsel spent the days leading up to Christmas helping Meghan see how important she was to both of her parents. The two of them talked about Meghan's favorite holiday traditions. Some of them would have to change because of her parents' divorce, but others—like driving around with her dad to look at Christmas lights at night, or enjoying hot chocolate with her mom while they read Christmas stories together wouldn't have to change in the least!

Once Meghan realized this, she began to enjoy the special holiday things that she could do with each of her parents. Just as Tinsel assured her, she was still the number-one priority for both her mom and her dad. This made Meghan feel safe and secure, even though she still had sad moments.

Tinsel also knew that it was important for Meghan to make the best of the situations she couldn't change. He helped her come up with fun new traditions to share with both of her parents such as building a gingerbread house with her dad and delivering it to a needy family along with a Christmas care package, and buying matching Christmas pajamas with her mom and wearing them while they watched holiday movies.

"Thank you, Tinsel!" Meghan told him on Christmas Eve. She and her mom were just getting ready to order Chinese takeout and play a Christmas board game that Tinsel had given them. This was another new, fresh tradition, and Meghan could hardly wait to get started.

"I didn't think I'd be able to enjoy Christmas this year!" she told Tinsel. "But thanks to a great friend like you, I think I'm going to be all right, after all."

Tinsel gave Meghan a squeezy-tight bear hug. "You sure are, Meghan," he said. "Merry Christmas!"

Christmas in a New Town

Tinsel the Chief Christmas Spirit Elf had a job that changed each year. He never knew exactly which boy or girl Santa would assign him to work with from one holiday season to the next. All he knew for sure was that whoever it was, he or she would be desperately in need of some Christmas cheer, and it was Tinsel's job to do the cheering-up!

This year, Santa sent Tinsel to a boy named Allan, who had just moved with his parents to a new city halfway across the country from the rest of their relatives and friends. Allan wasn't cheered up at all by the signs of Christmas all around him. They made him feel sad and depressed, reminding him of his relatives and old friends and what they had done together for past Christmases.

"Nothing is going to be the same!" Allan complained when Tinsel showed up at his house. "I don't have any friends around here, and none of our family is going to travel out here to spend Christmas with us. I wish I could just fast-forward the holidays this year!"

"Don't say that!" cried Tinsel. "Christmas isn't a lost cause, Allan. You'll have a wonderful holiday—just wait and see!"

"Yeah, right," mumbled Allan. Still, he couldn't help but feel a little bit flattered that Santa had sent one of his most important elves all the way from the North Pole to help him out. Was there a chance that maybe Tinsel could help him?

As Christmas got closer and closer, Tinsel played with Allan and became his trusted friend. When the other kids in Allan's new neighborhood saw Tinsel and Allan playing together, they decided they wanted to play, too. Thanks to Tinsel's encouragement, Allan soon had a whole block full of new friends!

Tinsel also helped Allan and his family by alerting them to the families in their very own neighborhood who didn't have plans or places to go for the holidays. When Allan's mom discovered this, she invited all of them over to her house for Christmas dinner! Everybody planned to bring something different, and Allan's parents spent hours getting ready for their guests.

Of course, Tinsel was in on the spirit of things, and he helped Allan's whole family decorate their house, bake Christmas cookies, and make other necessary preparations. It wasn't long before Allan was every bit as excited about Christmas as he had been back in his old home!

Although there would be a very different group of people around his Christmas table this year, and although Allan still missed his old friends and relatives, he had also learned the important truth that Christmas comes from the heart, and that it has the magical ability to make close friends out of perfect strangers!

"If it wasn't for you, Tinsel," Allan told him that merry Christmas Day, "I would still be sulking around. But you showed me that Christmas is still Christmas, no matter where it is or who it's with. Thanks for being a great friend, and for helping me make so many more friends, too!"

"You're welcome, Allan," smiled Tinsel. "Merry Christmas!"

Christmas Jokes

Q: Why does Santa go down the chimney?

A: Because it soots him!

Q: What do snowmen like most about going to school?

A: Snow and tell!

Q: What's Santa called when he takes a rest while delivering presents?

A: Santa Pause!

Q: When is a good time for Santa to visit?

A: Anytime!

Q: What songs do Santa's elves sing to him when he comes home freezing on Christmas night?

A: Freeze a jolly good fellow!

Q: Why couldn't the skeleton go to the Christmas Party?

A: He had no body to go with!

Q: How did the chickens dance at the Christmas party?

A: Chick to chick!

Q: Who delivers presents to baby sharks at Christmas?

A: Santa Jaws!

Q: Why is a cat on a beach like Christmas?

A: Because they both have sandy claws!

Q: Why did Rudolph wear sunglasses at the beach?

A: He didn't want to be recognized!

Q: What do snowmen eat for breakfast?

A: Snowflakes!

Q: What did they call Santa after he lost his pants?

A: Saint Knickerless!

Q: What nationality is Santa Claus?

A: North Polish!

Q: What can Santa give away and still keep?

A: A cold!

Q: How do sheep in Mexico say Merry Christmas?

A: Fleece Navidad!

Q: Where does Frosty the Snowman keep his money?

A: In the snowbank!

Q: Why is it so cold at Christmas?

A: Because it's in Decembrrr!

Q: What is Tarzan's favorite Christmas song?

A: Jungle bells!

Q: What's Scrooge's favorite Christmas game?

A: Mean-opoly!

Q: How does Santa Claus take pictures?

A: With his North Pole-aroid!

Q: What did Mrs. Claus say to Santa as they were looking out the window?

A: Looks like rain dear (reindeer)!

Q: Which reindeer has the worst manners?

A: Rude-olph!

Q: What does Santa call that reindeer with no eyes?

A: No-eyed-deer!

Find the Differences I

FIND
10
DIFFERENCES

Find the Differences 2

FIND
10
DIFFERENCES

FIND
10
DIFFERENCES

FIND
10
DIFFERENCES

Christmas Coloring Pages

33

FIND 10 DIFFERENCES

FIND
10
DIFFERENCES

FIND
10
DIFFERENCES

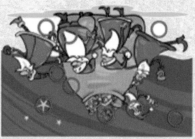

FIND
10
DIFFERENCES

About the Author

Arnie Lightning is a dreamer. He believes that everyone should dream big and not be afraid to take chances to make their dreams come true. Arnie enjoys writing, reading, doodling, and traveling. In his free time, he likes to play video games and run. Arnie lives in Mississippi where he graduated from The University of Southern Mississippi in Hattiesburg, MS.

For more books by Arnie Lightning, please visit:

www.ArnieLightning.com

36170817R00024

Made in the USA
Middletown, DE
25 October 2016